love of reading s

Every child learns to read in a different way and at his or her own speed. Some go back and forth between reading levels and read favorite books again and again. Others read through each level in order. You can help your young reader improve and become more confident by encouraging his or her own interests and abilities. From books your child reads with you to the first books he or she reads alone, there are I Can Read Books for every stage of reading:

SHARED READING
Basic language, word repetition, and whimsical illustrations, ideal for sharing with your emergent reader

BEGINNING READING
Short sentences, familiar words, and simple concepts for children eager to read on their own

READING WITH HELP
Engaging stories, longer sentences, and language play for developing readers

READING ALONE
Complex plots, challenging vocabulary, and high-interest topics for the independent reader

ADVANCED READING
Short paragraphs, chapters, and exciting themes for the perfect bridge to chapter books

I Can Read Books have introduced children to the joy of reading since 1957. Featuring award-winning authors and illustrators and a fabulous cast of beloved characters, I Can Read Books set the standard for beginning readers.

A lifetime of discovery begins with the magical words **"I Can Read!"**

Visit www.icanread.com for information on enriching your child's reading experience.

Library of Congress catalog card number: 2009930268
ISBN 978-0-06-184412-6
Typography by Rick Farley

09 10 11 12 13 LP/WOR 10 9 8 7 6 5 4 3 2 1   ❖   First Edition

I Can Read!™

READING WITH HELP 2

PLANET 51™

LEM SAVES THE DAY

Adapted by Gail Herman

HARPER
An Imprint of HarperCollinsPublishers

Lem felt great.

He had just gotten a job

at Planet 51's planetarium.

"This is just what I planned,"

he told his friends Eckle and Skiff.

"Soon I'll have a job,

a house, and a car," Lem said.

"Everything is going just right!"

Lem wanted his life to be

neat and tidy.

He liked having a plan

for everything.

But one day, Lem's life

was turned upside down.

A blaze of fire lit up the sky.

"Mom! Dad!" Lem said.

"There's a spaceship

in our yard!"

Lem saw something strange
race out of the ship.

"It's an alien!" Lem shouted.

He couldn't believe it!

Everyone on Planet 51

knew all about aliens.

Scary movies called Humaniacs

told them all they needed to know.

"This alien will turn us

into zombies!" yelled a man.

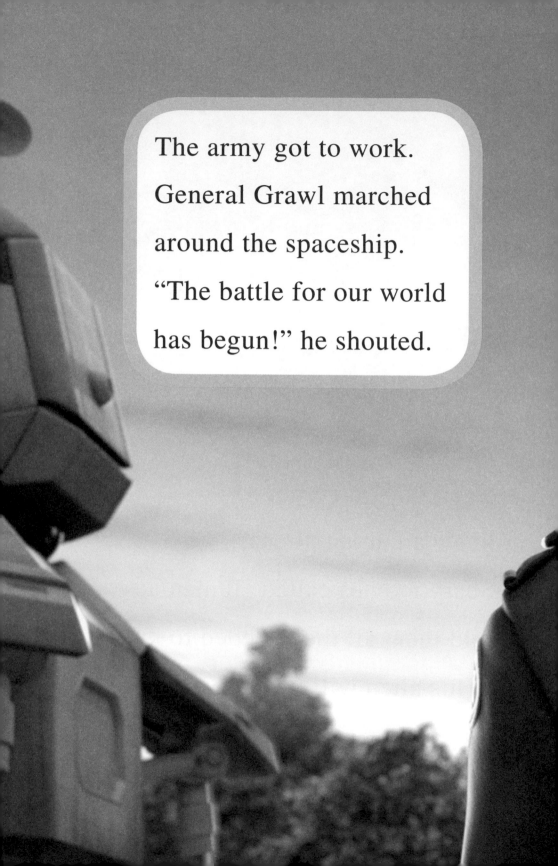

The army got to work.
General Grawl marched
around the spaceship.
"The battle for our world
has begun!" he shouted.

Lem worried about the alien,
but he had to get to work.
When Lem got to the planetarium,
he found the alien hiding there.
"Ahh!" Lem screamed.

"Ahh!" screamed the alien.

Lem ran one way.

The alien ran the other.

They raced across the round room

and ended up face-to-face.

"What do you want?" Lem said.

"I'd love a coffee," said the alien.

The two looked at each other.

They spoke the same language!

The alien's name

was Charles T. Baker.

He was an astronaut

from planet Earth.

He looked different,

but he seemed friendly.

Chuck had to get back to his ship.
But General Grawl's army
had it locked up at Base 9.
Chuck looked at Lem.

"Kid?" he said.

"Get me to my ship.

You're my only hope."

Lem thought about the danger.

He thought about his plan.

He could lose the job, the house,

and the car he had always wanted.

But Chuck needed him.

Lem had to help!

Lem had an idea.

The new Humaniacs movie

was showing,

and everyone was dressing up for it.

In his space suit,

Chuck looked just like

the aliens from the movie.

Lem led Chuck on stage.

Their plan was working!

Now they were

on their way to Base 9.

"Hey," someone said.

"That's not a costume!"

Chuck turned around.

"Uh-oh," he said.

Someone had figured out his secret!

"The alien must have turned Lem into a zombie!" someone yelled. "Get him! And get the zombie!"

Chuck looked at Lem and winked.

"Zombie! I free you!" he said.

"Go back to your life!"

Chuck had saved Lem.

But now Chuck was in trouble.

Lem had to find Chuck.

He and his friends

sneaked into Base 9.

They freed Chuck

before the general could stop them.

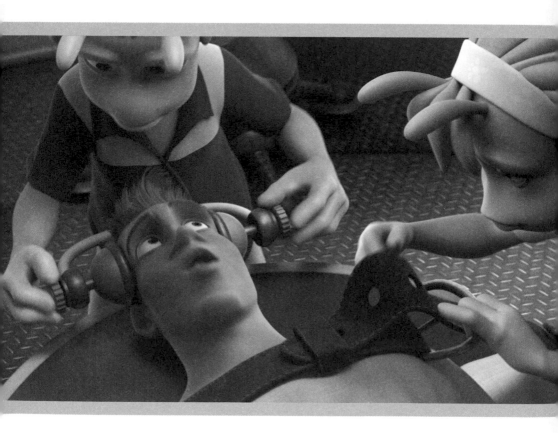

But Grawl wasn't ready to give up.

He held up a box.

"If I press this red button,

the base will blow up!" he said.

"Wait!" Lem told the general.

"You're only doing this because

you're afraid of the unknown.

I used to be scared, too.

But Chuck showed me

that even an alien can be a friend."

Lem smiled at Chuck.

"Time to get you home!" Lem said.

Lem grabbed the box

and pressed the red button.

The base was about to explode!

Lem and his friends ran to the ship.

But Grawl was knocked out!

Chuck dragged Grawl into the ship

just as a blast rocked the base.

BOOM!

The ship rose into the air.

Everyone was safe!

Lem had done it.

He had saved Chuck

and made a new friend,

all without a plan!

8